ST

FRIEND

STAR

FRIEND

Blessing,

Make a wish!

07/02/23

Gareth Baker

First published by Taralyn Books in
September 2015

4th Edition
© Gareth Baker 2019

Illustration by Haydn Cartwright
Cover from TheCoverCollection.com

For all the wishers and dreamers.

One

It was the start of the summer holiday, but Alice River was not excited at all. Usually she loved the long break, but not this year.

Alice was moving to a new house.

She had already said goodbye to her school, her teachers and her friends. Now she had to say goodbye to Lily, her next-door neighbour and best friend.

"I wish my mum never got this new job," Alice said to Lily.

"Be careful what you wish for, Alice," warned Lily. "Wishes sometimes come true. Your mum needs this job. Without it you'll have nowhere to live."

"I know, but I'll never have a friend as good as you. I may never see you again."

"We'll talk on the phone and the tablet," Lily kindly said. "You're not moving that far away. I can come and visit. It's not really goodbye."

Alice nodded and then felt her mum touch her shoulder. "Come on sweetheart, it's time to go," Mum said.

"Bye, Lily," said Alice

"Bye, Alice," said Lily.

Alice gave her best friend a hug and got in the car. As they turned the corner at the bottom of the street, Alice waved Lily goodbye through the window.

They drove away and after a while Alice curled up on the back seat and felt fast asleep.

When Alice woke up, her new home was right outside. She looked at it with bleary eyes. It was much bigger and older than she thought it would be. And posher.

It had three floors and lots and lots of windows. The front door stood under a porch that was held up by two stone pillars. You even had to walk up some stairs to get to it.

On the very top of the house, sat in the middle of the roof, was a glass dome.

Mum got out of the car and opened the back door. Alice leapt out onto the gravel driveway and looked around her. The house was sat in the centre of a huge garden. There were bushes, trees and flowers everywhere. It all looked a bit overgrown and uncared for, but Alice still thought it looked beautiful.

On the other side of the car, in the middle of the sweeping driveway, there was a huge statue of a man. A man in a skirt!

"Isn't it amazing here?" Mum said.

Alice smiled for the first time that holiday and nodded her head. Maybe it would all right here after all.

"Do we live in this massive house?" Alice said.

Mum smiled. "Yes, but not all of it."

"Who else lives here?"

"Mr Wallis. That's who I'll be working for. Now, I must warn you, Mr Wallis is..."

"Is what, Mum?"

"Let's just say he's a colourful character."

Alice looked at her mum. She did not know what she meant. The front door of the house rattled and Alice looked at it.

"Hello," boomed Mr Wallis as he stepped out into the light.

Alice's eyes stared in wonder. Now she knew what 'colourful character' meant.

Two

Alice stared at Mr Wallis as he walked out of the house.

He was wearing a skirt like the statue. It was made up of green, red and yellow stripes. On his feet he

wore sandals with brightly coloured odd socks. On his body he had a t-shirt that said *Save the Polar Bear* on it.

But his clothes, bushy beard and bald head were not the most colourful things about him. Neither was the round piece of glass that sat wedged in his left eye. It was the yellow snake that was wrapped around his neck and arm. It was also the chimpanzee that walked beside him.

"Hello," he said, in a voice so deep and loud that Alice wanted to cover her ears. "What's the matter? Have you never seen a man in a kilt before?" he said, patting his skirt.

"No, and I've never seen a snake before either," Alice said quietly, feeling nervous but still a little curious.

"Don't you be afraid of Candy, she's as sweet as her name and twice as friendly," Mr Wallis said, thrusting his hand towards her. It was huge and hairy. The snake's tail sat waiting on his wrist.

Alice hid behind her mum.

The chimpanzee hid behind Mr Wallis. Then he poked his hairy face between the man's hairy legs.

"Hello," Alice said, stepping forward.

The chimp blew a raspberry.

10

"And don't you mind this cheeky chimp either. His name is Charlie," said Mr Wallis.

"You're not cheeky. You're funny," Alice laughed.

"Nice to meet you again, Mr Wallis," Mum said, taking his hand.

"Please, call me Professor."

"Of course, Professor," Mum said.

A loud laugh split the air.

"I'm only kidding. You can call me Willie. I think you're going to fit in nicely here. Both Charlie and Candy like you, I can tell. What's your name?" he said, looking at Alice.

She told him her name and then gave him a dazzling smile.

"Nice to meet you Alice. I don't see the removal lorry I sent you."

"It's on its way," Mum said.

"Well," Willie said, clapping his hands and rubbing them together. "Come on inside."

Three

Alice followed the strange and wonderful man inside the house and into a large hall. Suits of armour guarded the open doors, and paintings of bald men and women in old fashioned clothes covered the walls.

Facing Alice was a large double staircase. She tipped her head back and looked up. The steps went on and on all the way to the top of the house. The ceiling above was made from the great glass dome she had seen from outside.

"I live on the bottom two floors. You'll live at the very top," Willie said.

Alice watched as Mr Wallis went over to a suit of armour and draped Candy over its metal shoulders. He kissed the snake on the nose and turned back to them.

"Now, I expect you'll want to see your new home," Willie said.

"It has been a long day," Mum said. "Mr River will be here soon. He's with the lorry. I expect they're running late."

"If you'll follow me then," Willie said.

Alice waited for the large man to get a few steps ahead of her and then followed, excitedly pulling Mum behind her.

At the top of the first flight of stairs Charlie rushed ahead and stood in front of a pair of doors. He spread his arms wide across them.

"These are my private rooms," Willie explained. "Only you and I will be allowed here. I meet all my guests downstairs."

"Of course, Professor W–, I mean, Willie."

"Good, good," he said, then carried on up the stairs.

Alice followed him and stopped by an enormous window that looked out of the front of the house. She could see her car, the statue and the drive. The gravel seemed to go on for miles and miles. So did the garden. And the fields.

"Excuse me, Willie," Alice asked. "But where does everyone else live? I can't see any houses anywhere."

"Everyone else?" Willie said, rubbing his smooth, bald head. "Oh yes, you're from the big city, aren't you? There's no one else around here. I own all the land as far as the eye can see. That's why I need your mum and dad."

"My dad? Why do you need him?" Alice asked.

"A little birdie told me that he doesn't have a job anymore and that's why you had to move."

Alice looked sad.

"Well," Willie said, "as well as a housekeeper, I need a gardener. I thought perhaps he'd like the job. What do you think?"

"I'm used to working in an office, but I'll take it," said a voice from behind them all. Alice recognised it straight away and turned around.

"Daddy," she cried, as she threw herself into his waiting arms.

"The front door was open so I let myself in. I hope you don't mind," said Dad.

"Of course not, Mr River. You've come just in time. Here…" Willie reached into his beard, pulled out a long, old-fashioned key and placed it in Alice's hand. "Well? What are you waiting for? Go and try it."

Four

At the very top of the stairs was another pair of doors. Alice moved the key towards the shining brass lock and slid it inside.

"Go on," Dad said.

Alice turned the key.

"Why don't we push it open together?" Mum said and put her hand on the door.

"That's a great idea," said Alice.

Alice waited for Dad to do it too and then she put her hand up.

"On three," Mum said.

Everyone nodded.

"Ready?" Mum said.

"One," said Dad.

"Two," said Mum.

"Three," said Alice.

They all pushed, and the double doors swung open. Alice gasped. It was amazing!

In front of her was a wide hallway that went all the way to the back of the house. There were three doors on each side. A window looked out across the back garden.

"Shall we explore?" Dad said.

"Okay," Alice answered, a smile spreading across her face.

She was off before her parents could say anything else. She ran to the end of the hallway and threw open the last door.

Inside was a huge room with its very own bathroom.

"May I have this room?" she asked.

"Okay," Mum replied. "We were going to let you choose first."

They explored the rest of the apartment. It was massive! Out the windows they could see the removal men unloading the lorry. It was squeezed in tight next to the statue.

"They were lucky they didn't hit that," Mum said.

"I don't think Willie would be very happy if they did," Alice agreed.

"We'd better go and help them," Dad said. "Alice, we'll get your stuff first."

"Thanks Dad. I'm just going to look at my room again and then I'll come and help. Honest."

"Sure, I believe you," Dad said with a smile as he left the room.

Alice ran down the hallway and looked out the large window. Then she went back to her room and started to imagine where everything would go.

A few moments later one of the removal men arrived with a box with her name on the top. Alice took it and started to unpack.

Five

Alice finished her unpacking by teatime and sat down to admire her new room. Suddenly she felt sad. She had no friends to share it with.

Alice walked into the kitchen where Mum and Dad were still unpacking.

"Mum, can I ring Lily please?" she asked.

"Of course, sweetheart."

Alice tried to call her best friend's mum, but there was no answer.

She waited a minute and tried again. There was still no answer. Then Alice had a better idea.

"Dad, can I use your laptop, please? I can show Lily my new room with the webcam."

"Of course. I've just unpacked it. It's on the table," he said.

Alice tried to video message her friend, but it would not work.

"It doesn't look like the professor has the internet," Dad said as he fiddled with the laptop.

"But everyone has the internet," Alice said.

"I'll talk to him about it tomorrow," Mum answered with a smile. "I think we need a break. Why don't we have a walk around the lake and then we'll come home and have something to eat."

"There's a lake?" said Alice excitedly.

"With an island smack dab in the middle of it," Dad said.

"Cool. Come on," Alice said with a big smile.

They left the house, explored the gardens and walked around the lake. It took a whole hour.

Alice kept looking at the island. It was covered in trees and looked even bigger than the house.

"Can you get to it?" she asked.

"I expect so," Dad answered. He pointed to a little wooden shed by the side of the lake.

"That's a boat house. I bet you can't guess what's inside it?"

"A car?" Alice said, pulling a face at her dad. "Can we go and visit the island now?"

"It's getting late," Mum said.

"And I'm starving," Dad added.

"Hmmm. Me too," said Alice. She looked up. The sun was setting, and stars were starting to appear. "Why can I see so many?"

"We didn't get to see them when we lived in the city because there were so many streetlights," Dad said. "I've got an idea. We could lie on the floor at the top of the stairs and look straight through the dome and up into the night sky."

"Cool!"

Alice ran home.

Six

"Alice, it's way past your bedtime," Mum said, poking her head out the apartment door.

Alice was still lying on the floor and looking at the stars. Mum and Dad had given up hours ago. The stone floor was cold, but Alice refused to get up, even to get a blanket.

"Just one more minute," Alice said, giving her mum puppy dog eyes. She waited for a moment to see if it worked.

"I suppose it is the holiday," Mum said as she laid back down on the floor.

"You start your new job tomorrow, don't you?" Alice asked.

"Yes. But look on the bright side — I'll never be far away, and neither will Dad. And you'll never have to stay at the after-school club ever again."

"I used to like going to after school club. Lily went too."

"Have you still had no luck ringing her?" Mum asked.

Alice shook her head.

"Try again tomorrow," said Mum.

"Okay."

"Right, off to bed," Mum said, and she started to get up.

"Look!" Alice cried, and pointed up through the dome.

"Wow!" Mum said.

A shower of shooting stars crossed over the dome, making the glass sparkle.

"Quick, make a wish," Mum said.

"Lily said wishes can come true," said Alice.

"Quick then, before they all disappear."

Alice smiled and said, "I wish for my best friend."

Mum smiled kindly before saying, "Right, bedtime, and don't forget to clean your teeth."

Alice wished Dad goodnight and disappeared into her bedroom. She put her pyjamas on, cleaned her teeth and then jumped into bed. She was just starting to feel warm and sleepy when she noticed that she had left the curtains open.

Alice climbed out of bed and closed the ones that faced the back garden. Then she went to the window near her bed. She was just about to pull them closed when another shooting star flashed past her window, filling the room with light.

33

"That's odd," Alice said. "That one seemed really close, like I could almost touch it."

Alice moved closer to the window and looked outside. All in darkness except for the moon and its reflection in the lake. The island in the middle of the water was just a dark blob, but something caught Alice's eye. There was something sparkling right in the centre of it.

Seven

Alice hardly slept all night. She got out of bed twice, crossed to the window and looked at the island. Each time the shooting star got dimmer and dimmer until, when she looked a third and final time, it was no longer there.

She got a science book, which her granny had bought her, from the shelf and found a page about shooting stars. They were not stars at all, but pieces of rock from space called meteors. As they fell to Earth, they got so hot they glowed like a star.

Perhaps she had dreamed it, Alice decided. Had she fallen asleep and woken up again?

*

In the morning there was a knock on the door. Mum popped her head inside.

"Good morning," she said. "If you get up now there'll be just enough time to make you breakfast before I go to work."

"Thanks, Mum," Alice said.

Mum had her usual breakfast ready and waiting.

"Right," Mum said, "I'm off. I'm so excited. I wonder what Willie likes for breakfast?"

"Have a good day," Alice called.

Mum left, and as soon as the kitchen door closed, it opened again and Dad walked through.

"Morning, Princess," he said.

"Have a great day at work, Dad."

"Thanks, Princess," Dad said as he blew her a kiss and disappeared back out into the hallway.

Alice waited until she heard the door to the apartment close and then she began preparing. She went into the cupboard, found an empty bottle and filled it with water. Then she grabbed an apple, an orange and a packet of crisps and took them all into her bedroom. Taking a backpack out of her wardrobe, she put the supplies into it then went into the hallway.

Alice opened the front door and peeked down the stairs in case Dad had forgotten something and was coming back. She sneaked downstairs and quickly walked past the professor's doors. Once on the ground floor, she checked the entrance hall was empty and hurried to the front door. It was time to see what was on the island.

Eight

Alice rushed along the outside of the house, ducking under the windows. She flattened her back against the wall and quickly looked around the corner. There was no one there, so she ran down the next wall.

When she reached the end, Alice stopped and looked across the garden. It was at least one hundred metres to the boat house. Luckily there were lots of bushes, trees and walls that she could hide behind.

Alice sneaked to the boat house, went inside and climbed into the boat. It wobbled underneath her as it rocked in the water.

With a big pull with both arms, Alice started to row the boat out of the house. Her arms began to ache, but she refused to give up. Soon the boat bumped onto the bank of the island.

That was when Alice realised that getting out of the boat without getting wet would be very, very difficult. She walked to the front and jumped out. Her feet splashed into the water and then sunk up to her ankles in mud.

"Great!" Alice said as she lifted her feet. They came out, one after the other, with a big sucking sound. She stumbled up onto the bank and fell to the hard, dry ground.

"Oh no," Alice said. One of her shoes was missing. "Just my luck."

Alice went quiet. She was sure she heard laughter.

Alice slowly turned her head to look and the laughing stopped.

"Who's there?" she called, her tummy suddenly full of butterflies.

When no answer came, Alice got up and started to walk into the trees. There was the snap of a twig and a blurred shape ran between the trunks ahead and hid behind one of the trees.

"Charlie? Is that you?" Alice called. "You are a cheeky chimp, aren't you?"

"Cheeky. Cheeky," came a squeaky voice.

"Who are you?" Alice called. Charlie might be cheeky, but he could.not talk.

"Poola. Poola," said the squeaky voice, and a figure stepped out from behind the tree.

Nine

Alice looked more closely at the stranger.

He was smaller than Charlie. His body was shaped a little bit like an egg. His arms and legs were short, and it looked like he had no fingers.

"Hello," she said.

"Poola. Poola."

They stood looking at each other and then the creature stepped out into a pool of light.

Two long ears sprung up from the top of its head, making it look a little bit like a rabbit.

"Poola. Poola," it called.

"Is that your name? I'm Alice."

"Alice, Alice," he repeated.

"No, I'm Alice. You are…?"

"Cheeky. Cheeky."

Poola took a step closer to Alice and reached out his arm towards her.

Alice copied him.

"Harm. Harm. No harm," he said.

"You're an alien!" she said. "So, I did see a shooting star. Or maybe it was your spaceship. Where is it?"

Poola moved closer and pointed at her.

"Alice. Alice," he said.

She nodded, slowly took off her backpack and opened it.

"Ziiiiiiiiiiip," Poola said, copying the sound it made.

Alice reached inside the bag and pulled out the orange she had packed.

"Food," she said, holding it up for Poola to see. Alice held her breath and waited.

He moved forward and his red nose twitched as he sniffed the fruit.

"Food. Food," Poola said.

"Yes," answered Alice, nodding her head. She dug her thumb into the orange and started to peel it. Once it was ready, she split the orange in two and then held out half to Poola.

"Food. Food," he said, taking it from her.

"Yum. Yum," she said.

"Yum. Yum," Poola repeated.

"Oh no," she said with a smile. "I'm starting to sound like you." Alice laughed.

Poola copied her and the sound filled her heart with joy.

Ten

Alice stared at Poola.

"Can you speak English?"

"Little. Little. Food. Food," Poola said, and then his arm dived into Alice's bag. Before she could say anything, it came back out with the packet of crisps.

"Noisy. Noisy," he said, as he rolled the packet between his hands. Poola put his nose onto the bright red bag and, pressing it to his face, sniffed it.

"Don't press too hard or—"

The packet popped!

"Ahhhh!" screamed Poola, throwing it into the air as he jumped back. Crisps landed all over the muddy ground.

"It's okay," Alice said.

"Okay. Okay," Poola replied. He picked up a crisp and lifted it to his nose.

"Don't eat it, it's been on the—"

Poola popped the crisp into his mouth.

"Yum. Yum."

"You like them?" Alice said in disgust and wonder.

"Like. Like," Poola said, thrusting another crisp at Alice's mouth.

"Er... no thanks, it's been on the floor."

Poola blew on the crisp, shrugged his shoulders and popped it into his mouth.

"Yum. Yum," he said, and gobbled up the rest straight off the floor.

"Don't do that," Alice said. "It's disgusting. You'll get ill."

"More. More."

"Really?"

Alice reached inside her backpack.

"I have an apple and a bottle of water."

"First. First."

"You want the apple?" Alice said, handing it over.

"Thank. Thank," Poola said, and pushed his paw finger into the top of the apple.

"No. No," Alice said. "That's how you eat an orange. With an apple you just bite it."

"Bite. Bite," Poola said. He brought the apple up to his mouth and started eating. Alice watched as Poola crunched and munched.

"Now," Alice said, "you can't live on this island. How am I going to get you home?"

"Home. Home. You friend?"

Alice smiled. "Yes, I am your friend."

Eleven

"This way," Alice said, as she walked back to the boat. Poola followed behind, but he had to skip to keep up.

"How cross? How cross?" Poola said, pointing at the lake.

"I came in a boat," Alice said. Then she noticed it was missing. The boat was floating in the middle of the water.

"Uh-oh!" said Poola.

"First I lost my shoe, now I've lost my boat."

"Shoe. Shoe."

"It's down there somewhere," Alice said, pointing at the muddy bank.

"Find. Find."

Before Alice could stop him, Poola waded into the mud. He dropped onto his tummy, stuck his paws into the brown, sticky stuff and began searching. He stopped and looked back at Alice. "You help?"

Alice looked at his muddy arms. His fur was absolutely covered! He even had it on his face. "I don't think so," she said.

"Find. Find," Poola said.

He turned back to the mud. It squelched and squished as his furry arms moved around in it. "Found. Found," Poola called.

With a loud sucking noise, Poola pulled his arm out of the mud and the shoe came free from the it's sticky grip, and from Poola's paw!

Alice watched the muddy shoe fly through the air and hit her on the chest. It stuck to her for a moment and then slowly slid down her body, leaving a long, brown stain behind it.

"Oops!" Poola said.

Alice looked down at her top and then at Poola. He was biting his bottom lip.

Alice laughed.

"Funny. Funny. Muddy. Muddy," Poola said, as he struggled out of the mud and stood on the bank.

"Yeah, great. Muddy," Alice said.

"You like?" Poola started to run towards her.

"No. No. That's not what I meant," Alice said, but it was too late. Poola jumped up into the air. He seemed to float for a moment and then landed in Alice's arms, sending them both tumbling into the mud.

Alice laughed as the pair of them rolled about on the ground. She lay on her back and stared up through the leaves as her laughter slowly died away.

"I can't remember the last time I laughed so much," she said.

"Fun, Fun," Poola said.

Alice found her muddy shoe and walked along the bank to a place that was not muddy. She washed her shoe clean.

"That's better. Nice and clean."

"Clean? You want clean?" Poola said from behind her.

"Yes," Alice said, looking down at her filthy clothes.

"I help," Poola said.

Alice felt something shove her in the back. "Wait! I meant the shoe!"

But it was too late.

Twelve

Alice tumbled forward and rolled into the water. She splashed around for a moment and then found that she could stand up. The water only came up to her waist.

"Fun. Fun," Poola shouted, and jumped into the air.

And stayed there!

He hovered in the air and did forward rolls that got faster and faster and faster.

Alice stared at him. "You can fly?" Alice said. "Is that how you shoved me into the water?"

Poola did not answer. He tucked himself into a ball and...

SPLASH!

Water went everywhere, washing off what little bit of mud was still left on Alice. She stood in the lake and let the water drain off her. "Thanks," she muttered.

"You welcome," Poola said. "Boat get?"

Alice looked down at her drenched clothes.

"Please, yes. I mean, yes please."

"I get," Poola said. He hovered above the surface of the water and moved out towards the boat. Alice stood in the lake and stared. He was amazing!

"Wait," Alice called, as she stumbled back onto the beach and grabbed her backpack. By the time she swam to the boat, Poola was already waiting inside it.

"Quick. Quick. Good swimmer," he said.

"So is your English. You're getting better all the time." Alice tried to climb into the boat, but it was too hard.

"I help."

"There's no way you can pull me in," Alice said.

"You wait," Poola laughed, and raised his arms up into the air.

"Wow!" Alice said. She was rising out of the water! She was floating in the air just like Poola. The little alien moved his arm and Alice moved away from the water and over the boat.

"How did you do that?"

"Just can. Can."

"Let's get home," Alice said as she was gently lowered down.

"Home. Home," Poola repeated. Alice thought he sounded a little sad.

Alice started to row, but she felt so cold from being in the water that it made her arms hurt.

Poola closed his eyes and raised up his arms.

"Wait? What are you doing?" Alice said. She had a bad feeling about this. But it was too late. The boat rose from the water until it was hovering a metre above the lake.

"Put us down, Poola! If someone sees us, we'll be in a lot of trouble."

"Trouble. Trouble," Poola laughed, and the boat started to move.

Alice sat and watched as the boat started to go around the island. "Lower us down!" Alice ordered.

Poola looked sad for a moment, but he lowered the boat. Alice looked over the side. They were just above the surface. Hopefully no one had seen from the house or the garden. She could not imagine how her mum and dad would react.

"Thank you," she said.

"Faster. Faster," Poola said, and the boat started to pick up speed.

Alice started to feel dizzy as the boat whizzed round and round. The island flashed past as they got faster and faster and faster.

"Stop! Stop!" Alice called. "I think I'm going to be sick!"

Thirteen

Alice let out a sigh of relief as the boat glided into the boat house and came to a stop. Poola lowered the boat back down onto the water.

"Now all I have to do is sneak you inside without anyone seeing," Alice said.

"Bag. Bag," Poola chattered.

"What about it?"

"Ziiiiiiiiiiip."

"You want me to open it?"

Alice took it off her back.

They had spun around so fast that it was almost dry again.

"Open. Open."

Alice did as he said.

"Now what?"

Poola did not answer. He smiled and climbed inside.

"You fit nicely," Alice said, "but you'll need to keep very still, like a statue, if we meet anyone."

"Poola like statues. Let me try," Poola said. His eyes stared straight ahead. His lips curled into a daft smile, the way Alice's always did in her school photos.

"Poola?" Alice said, but he did not answer. "Poola?"

"Ha. I trick you."

"Perfect. We need a code word so that if someone comes, you'll know when to do it."

"Statue? Statue?" Poola suggested.

Alice thought for a moment. "That won't work. I'll sound weird if I suddenly say 'statue'."

"What word you say when we meet?"

"Who's there?"

"No. No. Later," Poola said.

"Oh, you mean 'hello'," Alice guessed with a big smile. "That will work perfectly. Are you ready?"

"Yes. Yes."

Alice left the top of the bag open so Poola could breathe, then put it on her back. She quickly tied the boat up, climbed out and left the boat house.

It seemed that today was her lucky day. Not only did she have a new friend, but she managed to make it back to the front door without being spotted.

All she had to do now was get upstairs without bumping into anyone.

Fourteen

Alice quickly popped her head through the front door and looked around. The hall was empty except for the suits of armour and the paintings.

"We'll head straight upstairs, okay?" she said.

"Go. Go. Go," Poola answered.

Alice dashed across the tiled floor. Her soaked shoes squelched and echoed in the tall, empty space. She raced up the stairs and then slowed down again so that she could sneak past Willie's apartment.

The door opened and Alice nearly jumped out of her skin. Was it Mum or Willie?

"Good morning, Alice," boomed a deep, loud voice.

"Hello," Alice said, using the code word and quickly spinning around to look at Willie.

"I saw you on the boat out the window. I don't mind you using it, but make sure you're safe."

"Of course, Professor Wallis. I'll be careful."

"It looked like you were going very fast."

"I must have a special talent," Alice smiled.

"I could train you. I was in the Oxbridge boat race you know. You'd be unstoppable."

"It's been nice chatting, Professor Wallis, but I really need to get home."

"Have you seen your mother? I sent her downstairs to clean, but now I'd like a cup of tea. Perhaps I could make it. And one for you too, of course."

Alice smiled and hoped Poola would stay quiet.

"That's very kind, Professor Wallis, but I really need to get home."

"Are you all right, child? You keep calling me 'Professor Wallis'. Are you up to something?"

"Who? M… Me?" Alice said.

"Yes, you, Alice. What have you got on your back?" Willie stepped to one side so he could see the pack better. "What's this poking out the top? It looks like an ear."

"It's a cuddly toy. I found it on the island."

Alice froze. She could feel Willie pulling the top of the bag open.

"It's very hairy."

"Hey!" Poola shouted out. "Who you calling hairy, Baldy?!"

73

Fifteen

Alice wanted to run upstairs.

"It's alive!" Willie said. "What is it? Where did it come from?"

Alice sighed. She had been caught and she could lie no longer.

"A shooting star landed on your island and I found him there. I think I wished for him."

"Wished?" Willie said.

"Yes," Alice said, suddenly feeling foolish.

"He's amazing!" Willie whispered. Then he raised his arms about his head and did a little dance. "Quick, quick, come inside, and bring your little friend," Willie said, beckoning Alice to enter his apartment.

With a quick look over her shoulder to check Poola agreed, Alice walked inside.

"I've been all over the world and seen every creature on our beautiful, wonderful world. I've fed pandas. I've milked a yak. I've swum with dolphins. I've even been into the Himalayas to try and find the yeti, but I've never, ever, seen one of these. Please, will you let me see him?"

"Don't I get to decide if you can or not?" Poola said crossly.

"He can speak English," Willie said in surprise.

"Yes," said Alice. "And getting better all the time."

"I can speak Poolan too, so will you stop talking about me as if I weren't here," Poola said.

"Of course. I'm sorry," Willie apologised. "How rude of me. Let's go into the kitchen, get you out of that backpack and have a drink."

"Good idea," said Alice.

"Food. Food. And have food?" Poola said cheerfully.

"Of course," Willie said as he opened the kitchen door and walked in. Alice followed and put the pack on the floor so Poola could get out.

"That's better," Poola said.

"What do you eat?" Willie asked.

"What do you have?"

"What don't I have?! I have food from all over the world. I fell in love with so many tastes as I travelled the globe."

"Crips? Do you have crisps?" Poola said.

"Do I have crisps?" Willie laughed. "I make my own and experiment with different flavours. Would you like to try?"

"Oh boy, yes!"

"Okay," Willie said, "But first I have to get Charlie and Candy. They'll be very cross if they get left out."

Sixteen

Alice looked around the kitchen. They had been making crisps for over an hour and it showed. There were potato peelings everywhere. They were on the floor, on the work top, on the cupboard doors, and even on the ceiling.

The top of the oven had three frying pans on it. One was black from when it had caught fire. Oil was splattered everywhere. The kitchen was a mess!

Poola sat in the corner propped up against the wall. His tummy looked round and full. Charlie sat next to him and he looked full too. Candy was sat on the only clean part of the worktop.

"I think we might have over done it," Willie said. "Or at least, Poola has."

"Do you think it's safe for an alien to eat so many crisps?" Alice asked.

Willie rubbed his beard. "Make sure he eats plenty of fruit later."

"Me too," Alice said.

"Yes," Willie answered. "You do look a little ill. Oh no!"

"What is it?" Alice said.

"Look at the time!"

Alice looked at the clock on the kitchen wall. It was almost lunchtime.

"What's the problem? At least we won't need to eat anything," Alice said.

"But don't you see? That *is* the problem."

"Oh no," Alice said, just as she heard the door to Willie's apartment open.

Alice and Willie stood as still as statues and waited. Mum came through the kitchen door, let out a scream and dropped the feather duster she was carrying.

"What have you done to my kitchen?"

"Oh, chillax, Mrs River," Willie said. "We'll clean it up, won't we gang?"

"But, but, but…" was all that came out of Mum's mouth.

"There's nothing to worry about, Mrs River. I'll take full responsibility for the mess."

"But, but, but…" Mum said again. But this time she was pointing.

Alice looked. Mum was pointing at Poola.

"Hello Mrs River," he said.

Mum's eyes rolled up and she fell to the kitchen floor.

83

Seventeen

Alice and Willie carefully lifted Mum off the kitchen floor, carried her into the living room and put her in an armchair.

"Right, you'd better hide your friend before your mother wakes up," Willie said.

"Good idea, but what are we going to tell her when she does?" Alice asked, nibbling on one of her nails.

"Don't you worry. I'll think of something."

"Okay," Alice said, and went back into the kitchen. Poola and Charlie were cutting up more potatoes.

"I think you've had enough for one day," Alice said. She took hold of Poola's hand, led him out of Willie's apartment and up the stairs. She stopped outside her front door and slowly opened it.

"Hello? Dad?" Alice called, just in case he was home.

When no answer came, she rushed down the hallway and into her bedroom.

"I'm going back downstairs to check on Mum. Don't leave this room, and if anyone comes — hide."

Poola nodded his head.

Alice raced back downstairs and went back into Willie's apartment. Mum was awake and sitting up in the armchair drinking a glass of water.

"Ah, Alice," Willie boomed. "I've explained everything."

"Have you?" Alice asked, wondering what he had told her.

"I feel so silly," Mum said. "I thought I saw a little egg-like rabbit, but Willie explained it all."

"Really?" said Alice.

"It was the shock of all the mess," Willie said. "Your mum was so upset about it that when she saw Charlie her imagination just went wild."

"Yes," Mum said, taking a gulp of water. "Little furry balls of fluff with long ears just don't exist, do they?"

"No," answered Alice.

"I think your mum had better take the rest of the day off. Why don't you make sure she has a good lie down," Willie quickly suggested.

"But what about your dinner?" Mum said.

"Yes, what about dinner?" Alice echoed, staring at Willie and hoping he would get the message. Mum could not go upstairs, either.

"Oh, erm…" Willie said, realising his mistake.

"I feel so bad, what with it being my first day," said Mum. "But I think you're right Willie. Come on Alice, we're going home."

Eighteen

Alice sat with her mum in their apartment and watched television.

"You don't have to keep me company," Mum said with a yawn. "I'm a bit tired. I'm going to have a nap."

"Okay, Mum, I'll go and play in my room."

Alice went back to her bedroom. Poola was fast asleep in her bed.

"It must be catching," Alice said, yawning. Suddenly, the long day caught up with her.

She went and sat on her bean bag and fell asleep.

When Alice awoke, it was dark outside, and the curtains had been drawn. She had had a really weird dream. A shooting star had crashed on the island in the middle of the lake and there she found a fluffy alien who could float in the air and make other things float too.

Getting off the bean bag, Alice crossed to her bed. At the side of it was a plate with the leftover crusts of eaten sandwiches on it and a half full glass of milk. Alice did not remember eating them. In fact, she felt hungry.

Alice left her bedroom and went into the living room. Mum and Dad were sitting on the sofa.

"Hello, Princess," Dad said. "Have you just woken up? I came home and found both you and Mum fast asleep. Did you like the food I left for you? Your hair was all over your face, so I didn't wake you up."

Alice felt her mouth drop open. Someone *had* eaten the sandwiches.

And that meant it was not a dream.

Poola was real!

"Alice, are you okay?" Mum asked.

"Yes, they were lovely. Thank you. I, erm, just remembered something." Alice rushed away and flicked on her bedroom light.

The bed was empty!

"Poola? Poola?" Alice called in a loud whisper. She looked under the bed. She searched in the bathroom. She even checked inside the wardrobe. Poola was nowhere to be seen.

Suddenly a loud scream came from the other half of the apartment. It was Mum! Alice ran out of her room.

Alice burst through the door and found Mum had fainted again, only this time Dad had been there to catch her.

At his feet, Poola was busily munching a packet of crisps.

Nineteen

Alice stared at Poola as he shovelled the last of the crisps into his mouth.

"I'm starving, and these crisps are delicious. Do you want some, Alice?" Poola said.

"It talks?" Dad said. "And it knows your name?"

"He's not an 'it', Dad. He's Poola. He's from another world," Alice said angrily.

"What?" Dad said, as he carried Mum to the sofa. "Does the professor know you have a creature from another planet living up here?"

"Of course, he does. We made crisps together this afternoon."

"Crisps?" Dad said.

"Crisps. Yum. Yum. I love crisps," Poola said as he wandered into the living room, throwing the empty packet on the floor behind him and opening up another.

"This is what Mum was just telling me about. It's all true. Professor Wallis convinced Mum she'd seen Charlie, but it was… was this, wasn't it?"

"I told you, his name is Poola."

"Has he been in the kitchen all this time?"
Dad asked.

"No, Dad, he was sleeping in my bed
earlier."

"You mean when I brought that food in
earlier and I kissed you goodnight, I kissed
that?"

"Kissy. Kissy," Poola said, puckering up
his lips.

"He's my friend," Alice snapped.

"Your friend? He's out of here, that's what
he is. There's no way he can stay in this
house."

"I can't go back. Can't. I came here on a
magical meteor."

"It's true, Dad. I wished for a friend. I was lonely, and Poola came. It's magic!"

"Do you know what I wish? I wish HE wasn't here."

"That's a mean thing to say, Dad. Poola's the only friend I've got."

"You can't be friends with that. He's, he's…."

"He's what?"

"Not normal."

Alice looked at her dad and a tear slipped from her eye.

"I'm sorry, Princess. I didn't mean that. I meant—"

"I know what you meant, Dad. Come on Poola. I bet Willie will be happy to look after you."

But there was no answer.

"Poola?" Alice said. She looked around the room. She looked in the kitchen. She searched the whole apartment.

Poola was nowhere to be found.

Twenty

Alice lay in bed and cried.

Mum and Dad knocked on her bedroom door over and over again, but Alice was far too upset to talk to them.

First they took her away from Lily, and now they had sent Poola away. She had found the best friend in the world — in the universe even — and now she would spend the holiday alone.

When Alice woke up the next morning there was a plate of cookies, a glass of milk and a piece of folded paper next to her bed. It was a letter.

The people are coming later to connect us to the internet. You can speak to Lily. We've gone to work. Come and find us. We're sorry for frightening your friend away.

Love Mum and Dad

Alice put the letter down and ate the cookies. Then she drank the milk, put on clean clothes and brushed her teeth.

Alice slowly walked downstairs. Dad was outside. He was washing Professor Wallis's car. The statue seemed to be watching him, making sure he did a good job. Alice opened the door and stood under the porch.

"Good morning, Princess," he said with a sad smile, and threw the sponge he was using into the bucket.

"Morning, Dad."

"He couldn't stay. You know that, don't you?" Dad said with a smile.

Alice nodded, even though she did not agree.

"Hey, look," Dad said, pointing down the drive at a bright yellow van. "It's the engineer coming to sort out the internet. That's good, eh? You can talk to Lily."

Alice nodded. "I'm going to go and see Mum," she said, and walked back into the house. Through the window she could hear the beep, beep of the van reversing.

Alice started to walk up the stairs when she heard a terrible CRASH!

"What was that?" Alice cried.

She rushed back to the window. The tall statue wobbled backwards and forwards.

While the removal lorry had missed the piece of stone, the yellow van had not.

Alice tore open the door and shouted, "Dad! Look out!"

But it was too late.

Twenty-One

Alice screamed as the statue toppled back and smashed on top of Willie's beautiful classic car. She ran out of the house just as the engineer jumped out of his van. They both got to Dad at the same time. He was lying on his back, trapped under the statue next to the crumpled car.

"Dad? Are you okay?" Alice asked.

"Yes, I'm fine."

"Can you get out?" said the engineer.

"No. I'm trapped. Pinned down," Dad answered. Alice could tell he was just being brave.

Mum came running out of the house with Willie and Charlie close behind her. She came around the back of the car and put her hand to her mouth.

"It's all right, love," Dad said. "I'm not hurt."

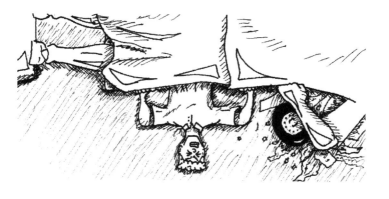

"Okay," Willie said, "No one panic. He's not hurt. When the fire brigade gets here, they'll get him free."

"I'm ring them now," the engineer said and wandered off with his phone.

There came a sudden, loud CRUMP!

"Oh no!" Alice shouted. "The statue's so heavy, it's squashing the car."

"Okay, okay. Don't panic. I was a weight-lifting champion at Oxbridge," Willie said.

"I thought you were a rower?" Alice said.

"All the same thing," he said, and put his arms around the statue. He heaved and he heaved and he heaved, but the statue would not move. "Let me try again."

"They're on their way," the engineer said, coming back from making his call.

"You," Willie said, pointing at the engineer. "Come and help me."

Alice held her Mum's hand and watched as the two men pulled and pulled on the statue.

Willie's face went bright red, but no matter how hard they both pulled, they could not lift the statue, even when Charlie joined in.

"We need someone with more muscle. We need someone stronger," Willie groaned.

CRACK!

Alice screamed as another part of the car squashed and the statue dropped even lower to the ground.

"If only there was someone else around. Someone who could help you lift it," Mum cried.

Alice smiled. She knew someone who could help. Someone who could lift the statue. And he loved statues. "I wish Poola were here," she whispered. Alice looked up and hoped for a bright flash across the sky, but there was not one. "He's not coming," Alice muttered, as a tear slipped from her eye.

BANG!

The old car seemed to scream in pain as the statue became too much. The car gave way and then…stopped.

"Here. Here," came the sound of a familiar, high-pitched voice from under the statue.

"Poola!" Alice cried, as tears of joy flowed down her cheeks. He had come! Even though Dad had sent him away, he had come.

"Back. Back," Poola said to Willie and the engineer. Then he raised his arms.

Alice could see the strain on her friend's face as the statue scraped across the floor.

"Come on, Poola," she cried.

The statue started to hover.

"Oh my," said Willie.

Mum covered her mouth.

The engineer just stared in amazement.

"Well done, Poola," Alice cheered, and she rushed to her dad's side. Alice and her mum grabbed his hands and pulled.

"I'm free," Dad shouted.

Poola moved his hand and the statue moved up.

"Hang on, I'll move the van," the engineer said. As it drove away, Poola moved the statue until it was back in its proper place. Everyone cheered.

"Oh no, your car," Alice said.

"It doesn't matter. Cars are just things, and things can be replaced, unlike friends and family. Isn't that right, Alice?"

But Alice did not hear.

She was too busy having a hug with Mum and Dad.

And Poola.

∎ ∎ ∎

Twenty-Two

Alice sat in the rowing boat next to her Mum, Charlie and Candy. Willie was rowing. He had lost an oar and was having to swap the one he still had from side to side to make the boat move.

"I thought you said you were in the rowing team," Alice said.

"It was a long time ago," he answered with an embarrassed smile.

Alice did not know what it was, but Dad had some sort of surprise waiting for her on the island.

A week had passed since Poola had rescued Dad. He had stayed for a couple of days, but then explained he had to return to his family.

The boat finally made it to the island and Willie made it stop next to a wooden platform.

"Dad made this jetty so you won't get covered in mud every time you come here," Mum said.

The three of them climbed out of the boat, onto the jetty and walked towards the trees.

Dad came out of the trees and stood in front of Alice.

"Are you ready for your surprise?"

"Yes, please," she said.

"Okay. There's one last thing," said Dad. "You need to wear this blindfold."

Alice let him tie it over her eyes and then she felt her Mum and Dad take one of her hands each.

"Come on," said Mum.

"This way," Dad added as they made their way through the trees.

"Now," said Mum. "Take off the blindfold."

Alice pulled it away. In front of her was a ladder that went up a tree.

"A treehouse!" Alice squealed.

"Go inside then," Dad said.

"Wow!" Alice was amazed. It wasn't just a tree house. It had chairs, a sofa, a carpet and a door. "What's through there?" Alice asked.

"It's another room. Why don't you go and look?" Dad said.

Alice opened the door.

"Surprise!" everyone called.

Inside Poola and Lily were sitting on a blanket covered with plates of food. There were lots and lots of crisps.

Alice smiled, made a silent wish and sat down with her two best friends. It was going to be the best summer ever!

117

About the Author

Gareth loves writing stories. He also loves old houses, lakes and islands. He hopes you enjoy reading this story as much he enjoyed writing it.

Gareth is a Patron of Reading

Remember, wishes can come true.

Make sure you visit

gareth-baker.com

Also available from Amazon as paperbacks and Kindle eBook

Signed copies also available from

gareth-baker.com

MOGGY ON A MISSION

Sometimes only CATS can save you

GARETH BAKER

Super Rabbit

Gareth Baker

Illustrated by Vicky Nolan

The Night I Helped
Santa

Gareth Baker

Find out more at

gareth-baker.com

Videos

Games

Activities

News

Sign up for the newsletter and get all the latest news

Please try to find some time to review this book on Amazon.

Thank You

Printed in Great Britain
by Amazon